Love Garden

Written and Published

By

Ashish Bhardwaj

ISBN- 978-93-5737-531-3

JAI SHRI RAM

ACKNOWLEDGEMENT

I would like to express my sincere gratitude to God for providing me with the gift of story-telling. I would also like to thank my parents for their encouragement and support throughout my journey as a writer.

I am also grateful to Mr. Inderjit Singh Saini for this title. I would like to extend my heartfelt thanks to all of the loved ones who have supported and encouraged me in my writing endeavours. Without their help, this book would not have been possible.

Lastly, I would like to extend a special thanks to Radhika, who was the first reader of this book and provided valuable assistance

ABOUT THE AUTHOR

Ashish Bhardwaj is a dedicated and dynamic teacher and storyteller who holds a Btech, MBA and runs an IELTS institute in Phagwara, Punjab. He is passionate about using storytelling in his teaching and has already published a book on the subject of IELTS Speaking, which has received over 100+ reviews on Amazon.

In addition to his work as a teacher and author, Ashish has also a YouTube channel to showcase his talent for engaging and inspiring others through storytelling. Ashish has a vision of transforming the education system and is dedicated to use his skills and passion to make a positive impact on the world.

Instagram - ashish_bhardwaj15
Youtube Channel- IELTS Speaking With Ashish

HERE WE GO

I was already running late for school. I asked my auto driver to speed up a bit but I knew, I wouldn't reach on time. As soon I touched the ground, I broke into a sprint. It was the beginning of the new session, and I did not want to be late on the very first day. As I was running, I saw that Aanchal was also standing in the line, and was pleading with the P.T teacher to grant her permission to go in the class. I took a moment to catch my breath, and then I joined her at the back of the line.

When my turn came, the P.T teacher asked "Why are you late?". I said "I missed my bus, so I had to take an auto to get to school".

He looked at me with a frown and then ordered both of us to stand still until he returned. I was happy, as I would get some alone time with Aanchal, but my luck ran out as he came back quickly, and said; "This time I am letting you both go but next time you will face consequences".

"Sorry Sir", we both said frantically.

Aanchal started walking hurriedly, followed by me. I

saw this as an opportunity and asked her why she did not come to school yesterday. She ignored me and started walking faster to reach the class. As she was about to enter the class, I spoke in a soft voice "Happy Birthday". She stopped there for the second and then entered the class.

I was very happy that day because I got the chance to wish her a happy birthday first. Although we were in the same class, we hardly talked. Aanchal was the topper and I was an average student. She had no interest in anything other than books, so I always looked for an opportunity to talk to her but always hesitated to do so because she was always busy with her books.

My name is Aditya and I am a senior in high school studying at St. John high school. I enjoy participating in sports and love playing football. In addition to sports, I also have a love for art and enjoy drawing in my spare time. It's a hobby that allows me to express myself creatively and relax after a long day at school. However, I keep my drawings to myself, as it's something that I do for my own enjoyment. This is the last year and after this I have to go to college. All the students in my class have extra pressure to do well in academics in order to get admission in reputed university, but not me. I have like no interest in studies.

I never expressed my feelings to her because I was afraid that I wasn't suitable for her. I fondly remembered the day I fell in love with the class topper. I was playing with my friends in a beautiful garden when I suddenly saw a beautiful girl in a bright red dress laughing and running. My heart skipped a beat because I had never seen a girl like her. I didn't recognize her at first, but my joy knew no bounds when I realized it was Aanchal, my classmate. I had never been attracted to her before because I had always seen her as a nerdy geek who was always into books. This was probably the first time I saw her in such a jovial mood.

She had long, black hair that flowed down her back in glossy waves. Her eyes were a deep, rich brown that seemed to sparkle in the light. She had delicate, refined features, with a small nose and full, rosy lips. She was tall and slender, with a figure that was graceful and elegant. She walked with a natural grace and seemed to float across the ground as she moved. Her smile was radiant, lighting up her face and causing her eyes to dance with joy. She was a vision of beauty, captivating and alluring.

It has been over six months since i realized that I

love her. At first, I thought it's just a crush but my feelings towards her grew deeper and deeper. I started visiting the garden regularly after my tuition's and soon i realized that she lives near the garden. I was ecstatic to find her house. One day I decided to visit the garden with my friends. We brought a football along with us and started playing. I intentionally threw the ball to her house so that she would come out and i could see her. But her elder sister came out and warned us not to play here. I apologized and returned back empty handed. Deepak, my most notorious friend in the group, somehow recall that she was Aanchal's elder sister as he has seen her in parent teacher meeting. He asked me that did I knew that this was Aanchal's house and was she the reason they're playing here. My face turned red and i had no clue what to say. With little more interrogation, I confessed my love towards Aanchal. That was my first mistake in the quest of finding love.

The next day in school, news of me liking Aanchal spread like a wild fire. Everyone was talking about us and in no time, Aanchal found about it and was very upset about it. I tried to apologize to her, but it added fuel to the fire, she became very angry and warned me to leave her alone or else she will complain about it. I had no choice but to let her go. This is the worst day of my life, i thought to himself. As days passed i tried to make amends with her but all in vain, she was not at all interested. This made me angry, and i picked a fight with Deepak, who was the main culprit, I started yelling and things quickly got ugly. The P.T teacher was informed and we were sent to the principal office. Later, we were sent home and were warned not to repeat this kind of behaviour on school premises.

I didn't know what to do but i kept on going to the garden at regular intervals, hoping she would forgive me, as I thought this has caused a dent in her reputation. One day, while I was looking at her window, i saw a big man staring me. I was petrified, I thought this was it, that this was how I was going to die. I started running and went straight home. I saw this as a bad omen and decided not to go the garden for few days. I decided to lay low for a while and not do anything stupid in school or in garden that might jeopardise my chances of getting together with her.

"Life sucks," I thought, kicking the pillow. All night, I had been dreaming about her and didn't know when I fell into a deep slumber. The next morning, when I arrived at school, I saw her talking to Vivek and

Rajat. This was very strange, as I had never seen her talking to boys before. I stood behind the pillar and listened to their conversation. Soon, I realized they were talking about some numerical problems in physics. This gave me an idea that in order to get close to Aanchal I needed to be in her league and be among the top five students of the class. However, this was not an easy task for me, as I was more comfortable on the football field than in the classroom. But this was my only chance to be friends with Aanchal. Hence, I was very happy and was motivated enough to improve my academics.

From the next day, I started sitting on the first bench and tried to focus more on my studies rather than day dreaming about Aanchal. My friends were shocked, as they have never seen this side of me. I ignored them and continued with my studies. It was a physics lecture and the teacher announced that there would be a test tomorrow and the marks of the test would be included in the end-term exam. I had never been serious about studies before, as I always thought of myself as a footballer, but this time it was different I had to prove a point to Aanchal. I Xeroxed the notes of the chapter from a friend, as I had never made my own notes and I pledged to score well this time.

I was ready to burn the mid night oil but as soon as I start studying I felt bored, and I found many of the topics to be overwhelming. But I didn't lose hope and I continued to study until 3.am. This was the first time I stay awake this late for studies, I was feeling proud of myself. The next day, I overslept and was late for school. But somehow, I managed to arrive at school just in time. The test was scheduled for the first period. As I entered the class, I saw the students moving around as the teacher instructed them to sit according to their roll numbers. I was very happy to see that my roll number was just ahead of Aanchal's, but she seemed pissed but I didn't care because my main focus was the test, not her.

The test begins and was difficult, and I find myself lost in my thoughts but I completed the test with head held high as this was the first time I worked hard for an exam. Aanchal on the other hand appeared confident. As the test ended, she gathered her belongings and returned to her bench. Excuse me, Aanchal, I said. She stopped and turned back. I said you forgot your pen, she took it and said thank you. I wanted to start a conversation but she quickly left. I was happy and thought that this was finally a positive response from her.

I was eagerly waiting for my test result and I don't have to wait any longer because the teacher brought our answer sheets with him. I have never been so nervous in my life and sir has a habit of distributing answer sheets by calling name and marks of the students. I my heard my name, Aditya. I was petrified, he said 12 out of 20 marks. He was impressed because my previous best score was only 5. But he was not the one who I intended to impress, I looked at her she seemed unmoved. Next, I heard her name being called Aanchal, 18 marks and sir congratulated her for being the topper and everyone started clapping. I was the loudest one, and she noticed it.

I was satisfied with my performance in the test, but I wasn't sure if it was enough to draw her attention towards me. I still felt way out of her league, and studying was not strong suit. Fortunately, the cultural fest was coming up in a month, and I wanted to do something to impress her. I decided to take part in painting and quiz competition. Painting was my forte, but nobody knew about it because I kept it. But, the only reason I choose to participate in the quiz competition was Aanchal, as she was also taking part in it. And, it was difficult for me to convince Mr. Rahul to allow me to participate in quiz competition but, I managed to convince him. After getting the permission from the sir I realize that I had about a 25 days to prepare for the competition, so I started reading as many books as I can.

I cut all ties with anything that would distract me from studying, and my visits to the garden became fewer as I focused on studying. It was a difficult three weeks for me, but I survived and finally, the day arrived and I was shivering because I didn't know what would happen. The fest began with the drawing competition; all the participants were called on stage. We were given one hour to draw. I started drawing the garden with Aanchal playing in it. I tried to remember every single detail of the day when I first fell in love with her in the garden and tried to put it in my drawing. I didn't win any prize, but my drawing was highly appreciated and I was very happy. I wanted to show my drawing to Aanchal, but she was nowhere to be found. Only a few minutes were left for the quiz competition, and her team was called. To my surprise, she was not on the team, and some other girl had taken her place. The quiz competition started, and I was not able to concentrate because my mind was on Aanchal. I was making a fool of myself on stage because I didn't say a single word. I was very embarrassed and didn't know how to react.

This had turned into my worst nightmare, and I just wanted it to be over soon. My team lost, and it was awful.

I returned home dejected and decided to visit the garden to catch a glimpse of her. I was late because I had to do some household chores. I reached the garden at 8pm and was shocked to see someone being hit by a reflection. I wasn't sure what was happening, but then suddenly I saw Aanchal crying. I tried to grab her attention, but it was all in vain because she closed her window soon and turned off the lights. I couldn't sleep that night because I was confused about why the man was hitting her and who he was - was he her brother or father?

Next day, she did not come to school and I became even more curious. I asked her friend Kanika why she didn't come to school, since she was usually very regular and hardly took any leave. Kanika replied that she didn't know. I had many questions in my mind and hardly any answers. I wanted to know more about her, so I forced Kanika to answer my questions about Aanchal. At first, she didn't want to talk about her, but I persisted and she agreed. I asked her why Aanchal was mostly into books and why she ignores me, without any reason, moreover I hadn't done anything to her. She said "she came here to study and that's all she is going to do- nothing else ".

I asked Kanika about her family, and she replied that she didn't know much because Aanchal is a private person. The only thing she knows is that Aanchal has a father and a sister. Then Kathy left.

I was not satisfied with the answers and decided to confront Aanchal the next time we met. But I had to wait two days because holidays were coming. I became helpless because I wanted to know if she was okay or not, and I didn't know what to do. The only option I had was to visit the garden and hope to see her there. I reached the garden around 9 pm, and it was almost empty. A few old men were sitting, so I sat at the end of the garden near the attic to see her again. I waited for almost 20 minutes, but then I had to leave because people became suspicious of why I was staring at the attic.

The only option I had was to wait for Monday. Finally, Monday came and I was very eager to reach school because I had a lot of questions for her. I entered the class and saw her sitting on the first bench solving math problems. I had a sigh of relief that she was okay. I don't know where I got the courage, but I went straight to her and asked her with authority why she didn't come to school on Friday. She was taken a back; she just shook her head and went back to solving math problems. I said, "I saw you crying. Why were you crying?" She was shell shocked and didn't say a word, but I could see in her eyes that she was about to cry. Just as I was about to say "I'm sorry," our teacher came into the class and I had to sit on my bench.

After attendance, the teacher asked Aanchal why she didn't come to the fest. She replied that her sister was ill, so she had to stay home to take care of her, and the teacher was satisfied with the answer. However, I was not. My plan to impress her with my studies had backfired, and now I had to do something else to be friends with her. I remembered that I still had my drawing with me because I hadn't won any prize, so they returned it to me. I wanted to give it to her, and soon I got the opportunity. She was sitting alone and was writing something in her journal. As soon as she saw me, she got conscious and hid it from me. I said, "I'm sorry for yesterday," and handed her my drawing. She seemed curious because she had no idea what it was. She took it and looked towards me with a smile, a silent thank you! I acknowledged it with a crooked smile.

I said "hi," to which she replied, "You're crazy!"

But my parents told me my name was Aditya. I replied with a witty smile.

This was by far my best day, and I thought to myself that my love story had begun. Every single day we both shared a smile, and that was it. I tried to strike up a conversation with her, but she would ignore me every time. I was confused by her behaviour. One moment, I thought she liked me, and the next, I was a complete stranger to her. Our exams were approaching, so I thought she wanted to concentrate on her studies and would talk to me after the exams. I decided to let it go and just wait.

I started preparing for exams as I also wanted to score good as I didn't want her to be embarrassed by her boyfriend (which I hope I was). Soon our exams were over and I brought a chocolate for her as a present. I didn't get the opportunity during the school hours so I decided to give her after the school. I saw her waiting for someone at the school gate as I was approaching her she saw me and just turned the other way around, I was still walking towards her, then suddenly the same big man with a grin on his face asked her to follow him she didn't utter a word and followed him and then they both sit in the car.

I had a feeling that her father was strict and that was the reason she didn't want to talk to me. Our exams were over, and we had a break for 10 days. I wanted to talk to her, but I didn't know how. I went to the garden that night, hoping to catch a glimpse of her, and I was lucky. I saw her near the window, writing something in a notebook or journal. I tried to catch her attention, and I was successful. She saw me and smiled. I made a gesture of a phone to ask for her number, but she didn't respond and shut her window drapes. I got upset and decided not to visit the garden again. Four days passed, and I didn't go there. I received a call from Lakhan, my classmate, who said Kanika wanted to talk to me. I was surprised, but I agreed.

Hi Aditya!" said Kanika. "Hi!" I replied.

"I want to talk to you about something very serious," she said. "I'm listening," I replied. "Aanchal wants to meet you and it's urgent." I was happy and asked her what the matter was, but she replied that she didn't know. She told me that Aanchal was coming to her house the next day and I could come at 5 o'clock to meet her. I was ecstatic and couldn't sleep that night because I was busy dreaming about the next day. I was considering all the possible outcomes and didn't know when I fell asleep.

Next day, I wore my favourite jacket and jeans. I bought flowers and chocolates for her. I arrived on time, and Kanika's house was not far from mine. I was waiting for Aanchal and Kanika, but I could only see Kanika. I asked Kanika where Aanchal was, and she replied that she couldn't make it because she had some work to do. I was flabbergasted and angry, as that was not what I was hoping for. I threw the flowers on the ground and started walking back. As I was walking back, Kanika called me and said she had a letter from Aanchal for me. I was very intrigued and took it from her. I also gave her the chocolates I had bought for Aanchal as a thank you, and then I returned home.

I was very excited to read the letter. The letter was covered in an envelope, I tore down the envelope and opened the letter my most prized possession. I was very nervous and started reading.

Hi Aditya,

I wanted to tell you this in person, but I couldn't, so I am writing you this letter. It's been over six months since you have been following me around. You almost regularly visit the garden, and you try to make contact with me at school. You are a very nice guy, and any girl would be happy to have you as her boyfriend, but I am not that girl.

I want to thank you for the beautiful drawing you made for me. It was the most beautiful gift anyone has ever given me. But for me, my career is my first priority. I can't risk jeopardizing that.

I am sorry. Take care, Aditya. You're a sweet boy. Aanchal

I had tears in my eyes when I finished reading the letter. I was very disappointed and decided to forget her, as she didn't want anything from me. There were still five holidays left, and I was not in the mood. So, I decided to visit my grandparents. Their house in our village is the place where I feel perfectly content. It is not just a place, but the heart of my family. Though we currently live miles away and only visit it every summer, it is still the best place on earth to me, where I cherish very gratifying memories.

The house is small, with three bedrooms. The front door of the house is connected to the garden gate, with a huge open space leading to a set of concrete steps. These concrete steps are where all of our cousins gather. We would sit for hours, exploring the innumerable stars in the sky and sharing and caring with each other, relishing the delicious dishes made and served by the superwoman of our family, my grandmother. Those immensely treasured moments are cherubic and eternal in my memory.

During my first few days, I was numb and didn't know what to do. I was lost in my own thoughts, dreaming about Aanchal, but I promised myself that I wouldn't think about her. I want to move on from her and this was a trip that could help me in achieving this. I really enjoyed my time there and I felt fresh and rejuvenated, but I didn't want to come back. However, I had to because the holidays were over.

The next day, when I reached school, I completely ignored Aanchal. It was very difficult for me, but I did it. At lunch, Kanika came to me and asked about the letter. I said, "It's none of your business." She was very interested in knowing my reaction, but somehow, I ignored her as well.

A few days passed and I was ignoring Aanchal. It was killing me inside, but I didn't have any other option. One day, I saw Aanchal looking at me and we made eye contact. We both were staring at each other, as if we were looking into each other's soul. In no time, I saw tears in her eyes and she started looking in another direction. I was confused. Why was she playing with me? If she didn't have any feelings for me, why was she crying? I wanted to talk to her, but she always avoided me.

One time, she was sitting in the class alone reading something. I grabbed her by the arm and asked her what the hell is happening. She replied with a trembling voice, "Leave me alone." I didn't care much and asked my question again, looking directly into her eyes. She didn't say anything and started crying. I didn't know what got into me, but I kissed her. She pushed me away with both hands and gave me an angry look. I said, "I love you, Aanchal." She slapped me and went outside the class with her handkerchief, hiding her tears.

I was numb at that moment and didn't know what the hell had happened. Then, I heard some footsteps and a shrill voice belonging to Kanika, asking me what had happened and why I looked like someone who had seen a ghost. I couldn't reply to her and asked her to leave me alone. I wasn't able to concentrate the whole day. I just wanted to go home because I couldn't digest what had happened that day.

Aanchal didn't come to school the next day, and I was very worried. The only person who knew something about Aanchal was Kanika, and my behaviour with Kanika had not been good in the past few days because I had talked rudely to her more than once. So, when I tried to have conversation with her, it was her turn to be rude, but I begged her because I was desperate to know about Aanchal. She then broke down and told me that Aanchal was going to shift to some other city and was going to leave school in the middle of the year. The thought of not seeing her daily killed me. I asked her how it was possible to leave school in the middle of the year. Kanika said that due to her previous records and a reference from our school, she could get admission in the middle of the year. I was shell-shocked and couldn't control my tears. I asked Kanika to give me some private time, and she was kind enough to leave after giving me a sympathetic hug.

I just wanted to go home and cry. Sometimes, things are always worse than they seem. I got lost in my mind and wasn't thinking straight. I tried to sleep to escape reality, but no amount of sleep in the world could cure the tiredness I feel. I was scared to tell people how much it hurts, so I decided to keep it to myself. But it was getting harder to hide the pain. Monsters don't sleep under your bed; they scream inside of your head. That's exactly how I was feeling. The excruciating pain of not seeing her was killing me. I just wanted to feel okay again. Death seems more inviting than life. I wasn't myself anymore, and it sucks when you know that you need to let go but you can't.

I didn't go to school for a few days because my world was upside down. I told my mom that I was sick and wanted to take a few days off. She agreed because my exams were over, so she didn't raise any eyebrows about my decision. I was ignoring everyone and just wanted to be alone. But after three days, Lakhan came to my house. He was very keen to meet me, but I wasn't. He told my mom that he had something very important to tell me. I didn't want my mom to be suspicious, so I agreed to meet him.

I was not in the mood for any assignments or study-related emergencies. But I was in despair when I heard what he had to say.

He said Aanchal is missing... she is nowhere to found.

I said what... Aanchal is missing. How can that happen? I couldn't control myself and started crying. Lakhan said he was sure Aanchal hadn't returned from school yesterday and that the police had come to the school today to inquire about her. My initial reaction was to beat the shit out of Lakhan for joking about such a serious matter, but he seemed unmoved. I thought to myself that the unthinkable has happened. He said I needed to come to school tomorrow as the police wanted to investigate the matter. I asked him if this was a case of kidnapping and if there had been a ransom call. He replied that he didn't know; he had just come to make sure that I would come to school tomorrow. Later, in the evening I decided to visit the garden at night to be sure, and when I arrived at the garden, it was a terrible sight. I saw Aanchal's sister crying and her father talking to a police officer, with many people standing outside her house.

The news of Aanchal's abduction was in all the local newspapers the next day. It was not a usual day at school. There was an eerie silence in the school building. When I reached my class our teacher instructed every student to go one by one to the principal's office and have to answer a few questions asked by the investigation officers. We all said, "Yes, ma'am," and then I saw Kanika crying. She was unable to control her tears. I asked the teacher if there was any news regarding Aanchal. She replied in the negative. I could sense disappointment in her reply.

One by one, students were called into the office. When it was my turn. I was shaking with fear, all I wanted was for Aanchal to be well. When I entered the office, I noticed the principal had a grin on his face, and an unfamiliar face was sitting next to the principal. I reckoned he was from the police department. Then, the principal started asking questions about Aanchal, like what kind of relationship I had with her and how much I knew about her. I was petrified and told the truth. I said I liked her and didn't know much about her, as she was a private person and we hardly talked. Then the officer asked why I often went to the garden near her house. I wasn't sure what to say; I just said I wanted to see her. Out of the blue, his next question was, 'Where is the letter?' I was surprised. How did he know about that? I said I had the letter with me. He asked me to bring the letter, and I had it in my bag, as I didn't want the letter to be caught by my mother. When I came out of the office, I saw Kanika crying, and it didn't take me long to guess that she was the one who told the police about the letter. I brought the letter, and I was asked to leave for the time being.

Two days passed and there was still no clue of Aanchal. I couldn't sleep or eat. All I did was pray for her well-being. The next day, I got a call from Kanika. She was crying inconsolably, and I didn't know what had happened. I asked her to calm down and tell me what happened. Then she broke the sad news to me: the body of Aanchal was found near the dumping ground. I said, 'What?' She replied, 'Aanchal is dead, Aditya! She's not with us anymore.

I didn't know how to react, and I disconnected the call. I was in complete denial. 'This can't be happening to me.' I started bargaining with God: 'Make this not happen, and in return, I will go to temple daily.' I was very angry with myself. I didn't know why this was happening. All questions with no answers. I started running to her house to see it for myself. As soon as I reached, I saw her sister crying. Her house was filled with people, and all of them were crying. Then I saw the most horrific thing I thought I would never see in my lifetime. I saw her dead body covered with white cloth and her smiling picture on the wall in front of which her relatives were crying. I broke down there. Lakhan saw me there and picked me up, taking me back to my home.

The news of her death spread like wildfire. All the newspapers were filled with this horrific news. She had a severe head injury which resulted in her sudden demise. It was mentioned in the news that she was neither molested nor sexually assaulted. Our school declared holidays for two days, as they didn't want any eyebrows raised at them.

This was surely a murder case, but the police were not sure what the motive was, as there was no call for ransom and she was not even sexually molested. The police found this tough nut to crack. I was not in my senses as I couldn't believe what had just happened, so my parents decided to send me to my grandparents for a few days. As we were planning to leave, a police officer came into our house and asked for me. He said I was called in for an investigation.

For now, I was the only suspect because I had been the only one stalking her in school and at home. Her neighbours testified against me, as they had seen me many times in the garden looking at her window. At school, everyone knew I liked her, and she didn't. The letter added fuel to the fire. The police were under immense pressure, as this case was getting national attention, so I was made the scapegoat and considered the prime suspect. I was asked not to leave the country without informing.

My life was officially a living hell now. I had lost the love of my life, and I was the prime suspect in her murder. I wanted to die at that moment. Death was the only possible solution I had in my mind. My parents were looking for a good lawyer, which was very hard to find, as I was portrayed as a criminal who murdered an innocent girl. I was drowning fast in this mess. I just wanted to sleep, I thought to myself. Aanchal is waiting for me on the other side, and I had to reach her. I decided to commit suicide, as I was about to do something stupid. I heard my mom cry, and she came running to me. She said the real culprit had been caught and I was a free man now. I didn't know whether to be happy or sad. I was numb and had tears in my eyes. After gaining my senses, I asked my mom who it was.

To which she replied it was her father. I was shocked to my core when I heard this. I was like what... how can a father killed her own daughter. Even father daughter relationship is tainted. As I was thinking about this I got a call from the police department that I was called in for some formalities.

When I reached the police station, I saw Aanchal's sister crying, and the police officer apologized to me for the inconvenience. I said it was okay, he was just doing his duty. I asked him how the case was solved, and he handed me a diary and a letter. When I saw the diary, I quickly realized it was Aanchal's, as I had seen her holding it many times. I asked him why he was giving it to me, and he replied that it belonged to me. I was about to open the book when I suddenly heard the voice of Kanika. I was surprised to see her there.

The police officer said that she was the one who helped them catch the real culprit. I asked him how, and he said that the letter which she gave me was not from Aanchal; it was written by her. I looked at him with disbelief and asked why she would do this.

Suddenly, I could hear Kanika crying. I was confused and asked if anyone could explain to me what was happening.

The police officer started explaining. He said Kanika liked me and had a crush on me. She didn't like the fact that I loved Aanchal and was always jealous of her. At first, Aanchal didn't like me, but over time she developed feelings for me, which she told her only friend, Kanika. Kanika knew about her family and knew how strict her father was, so she convinced Aanchal to stay away from me or else she would have to face his wrath if he found out about their love affair. So Aanchal agreed to stay away from me for the time being. But I continued to fall for her, and she was unable to control her feelings for me. Hence, she decided to meet me in private to explain her love for me and asked Kanika to help her. Kanika didn't like that at all, but she agreed. Then she convinced Aanchal to write a letter instead of meeting, as she said her parents wouldn't allow her to have a guy friend at home.

The letter which you had was written by Kanika, and the letter which I gave you was written by Aanchal. I was shattered and asked in a trembling voice how they came to the conclusion that her father killed her. The police officer said that when they were examining the letter as evidence against me, they found that the writing in the letter was different from Aanchal's normal writing and concluded that the letter was not written by Aanchal. Before confronting me, they confronted Kanika, as she was the one who had handed you the letter. She broke down and confessed everything. She said that the original letter which Aanchal wrote for me was replaced by her own letter written for you, in which you were asked to stay away from Aanchal.

You did that, and it was hurting Aanchal. One day, when you kissed Aanchal in class, Kanika saw you and got very angry. She wanted to get back at Aanchal, as she already possessed the original letter. So she took a Xerox copy of the letter and decided to give it to Aanchal's father, while keeping the original with her. In the meantime, Kanika's cries were getting louder and louder. She was pleading that she never knew Aanchal's father would kill her; she just wanted to break us up and was very sorry for what she had done. I was shivering and crying inconsolably. The girl I loved the most loved me too. I didn't know whether to be happy or sad. For all the time, I thought I was the only one who was in love.

I asked the officer how a father could kill his own daughter over something so petty. He looked into my eyes and said he was her stepfather. When the police found out about the letter being given to him, but he still didn't tell them about it, their suspicion grew. They started investigating the matter in a new direction and, when they searched the house, they found Aanchal's diary in which she mentioned how afraid she was of her father. But the letter was nowhere to be found. As he had destroyed the letter, but he didn't destroy the diary, as he didn't know such a diary existed. He was then interrogated and he confessed to his crimes. He said that when he read the letter he got very angry and started drinking and then hit Aanchal with a lamp and she felt unconscious on the floor and then he locked the door. Due to bleeding Aanchal lost her life. Next day he himself cleaned all the mess and then dropped the body at the dumpster.

I am really sorry Aditya, I wish could I do something for you. The officer said.

I just want to go home, I was not crying at that moment. I said, and picked up the letter and the diary and went home. My parents were also there they didn't said a single word nor did I. I went straight into my room and locked the door. I didn't have the courage to read but I had to, I wanted to know her. I slowly opened the letter. Tears were flowing down my eyes when I began to read.

Hi ADITYA

"Knowing you is the greatest thing that has happened in my entire existence. I never realized how happy and complete I feel when see you by my side. You don't even need to do anything. The thought of you staying by my side reassures me and gives a whole new meaning to my life. When I gaze into your soulful eyes, I can see a brighter tomorrow. Your beaming smile chases all my worries and uncertainties away. The moment that I saw your drawing of me, I knew right away that you are the one I want to spend the rest of my life with.

No words could ever express the joy that I'm experiencing right now. I even start to realize how blessed I am to have you in this life. In any other lifetime, I would still choose to fall in love with you. I thank God for bringing you into my life. You gave a new meaning to my existence and I cannot imagine a life without you in it. You and I were meant to be together, forever. Loving you was the most special thing that ever happened to me. You have a very special place in my heart and no one could ever replace that, whether in this lifetime or any other lifetime.

I will never leave you and you will always be my knight in shining Armor. I'm willing to go against anyone who wishes you harm. This will be my vow from now until eternity. I will never leave your side. I'll always be here my sweet love.

I am deeply in love with you and if given another chance, I'd still choose to fall in love with you. I never thought that I could meet someone so amazing. I'll never let you go. I have never been this sure in my entire life. I have never felt this way with anybody else. And I want to celebrate this deep love with you.

But there are many things which you still don't know about me and trust me when the time is right, I will tell you every single detail of my life. Till than I just want you to know I love you and one day we will be together.

AANCHAL

As I finished reading, I had tears in my eyes. I didn't know she loved me. I thought she liked me a bit because we used to stare at each other sometimes, but I didn't know about her undying love for me. I cursed God for taking her away from me. The next thing I had to do was read her diary, even though I didn't want to because I didn't have the energy. I was in emotional hell, but I had to do it.

Her diary had a title
Open the darkness, I am home....

MARCH 15,2004

I'm Aanchal. It's my birthday today. I turned 12 today. But as usual, I'm not happy. I miss you, Mom. It's been 8 years since you left me and Radhika. I miss you every day. I don't have anyone to talk to, so today I am going to write everything I feel in this journal and I'll think as if I'm sharing it with you. I hope you are watching me and showering your blessings from up there. I have very faint memories of you, but whatever I remember is the only thing that gives me happiness.
I MISS YOU.
AANCHAL.

MARCH 18, 2004

"I lost my father when I was 3 and my sister was

7. In order to survive in this cruel world, my mother had to marry again, and that was her biggest mistake. Her new husband was a drinker and always looked at me and Radhika with dreadful eyes. But my mother was there to shield us from him. However, one day everything changed. My mother was diagnosed with cancer and it was the last stage. We tried everything we could to save her, but since it was the last stage, nothing could be done and eventually she died. She just left us here in this cruel world with our stepfather, who never loved us. I was 4 at the time you died. I never understood where you went. I was told that you went to live on the stars and that you would be watching us every day from up there. I got angry at first and asked why you left us alone here, why didn't you take us with you, and why you never returned my calls or wrote to us? I used to cry a lot, and whenever I asked about you from my stepfather, he would first beat me up and then lock me in a dark room, leaving me there for the whole day, starving. He never took me out of that room. It was always Radhika who would come to my rescue.

As I grew a little older, I understood that my mother was dead and she was never coming back no matter what. I stopped asking about my mother from my stepfather or about anything else too, because whenever I opened my mouth about anything, he would beat me and eventually lock me up in the room. I became very quiet day by day. I wanted love, but I couldn't get any. Radhika was the one looking after me. She always tried to cheer me up, play with me, help me with my studies, and tried to talk to me to share what I was feeling and going through, but she never shared herself. Many times, I saw her crying alone. My stepfather used to beat her up too, but she never complained. She kept quiet in order to save me from him. Although my sister and I shared less, she always tried to cheer me up. She advised me to study hard and become independent in order to start a new life away from this hell of a home. My stepfather forced her to drop out of school in order to stay at home and take care of me and him. It was just because he didn't want to spend all his earnings on our education (because then he would have nothing left to drink) and Radhika wasn't even good at studies. But he let me continue because I was a bright student from the start.

My stepfather never talked to me or liked me asking him about anything. But whenever he saw me sitting idle or playing, he would beat me and tell me to study and that he's not paying my school fee for me to play or enjoy, but to study. Whenever I used to get the first position in class, he never appreciated or congratulated me. But when I got less marks, he would beat the crap out of me. He never even allowed us to go outside and play with others because I think he was scared that we would tell someone about him. But Radhika used to take me out and play with me whenever our stepfather wasn't at home. There's a very beautiful garden in front of my house. I remember my mother used to take us out every evening and play with us there when she was alive. But after she died, things were not the same as they used to be.

25 JULY, 2004

I'm really happy today. There was an interschool quiz competition and our school secured the first position in it. It feels like my hard work is paying off. I was appreciated the most for my overall performance in the competition and have been awarded a scholarship for the next year. Radhika was so happy for me. She even made me my favourite rice pudding. She told my stepfather about it, but he didn't pay much attention. I felt bad because he didn't appreciate me, but I am really happy today after a long time and feel like I have started to walk towards my path of achieving something big.

FEBRUARY, 2005

It was a horrible day. I can still hear Radhika's loud, terrifying cries of pain. My father beat her up today. I just can't understand why he hates us so much. We were just sitting and talking to each other, like most sisters do, but as soon as he saw us chatting, he locked me up in my room and started beating Radhika. I could feel her pain. She was crying a lot and asking him to forgive her, but it was all in vain. He kept beating her until he was exhausted. I wonder what kind of man likes beating his daughters up and leaving them in tears. After all, we were never really his daughters.

15 MARCH, 2005

It's my birthday today. I turned 13. Happy birthday to me. I hope everything goes well today. But I hate the day I was born. I don't want to live in this world. I hate myself. I hate my father. He's a monster. I was so happy today. I thought my life had finally started to get back to normal, as I made some friends at school in the new session. I was even doing well in my exams. I found solace at school, reading books, playing, and studying. School was like a home to me. I had no idea my friends had planned to give me a surprise today, since it was my birthday. They suddenly came to my place after school and surprised me with a birthday cake. I felt so happy in that moment and forgot everything about what I've been going through in my life. But as they say, all good things come to an end. My father came home early and saw my friends at our place. He didn't say anything at the time and went outside again, but I could sense the anger in his behaviour. I somehow asked my friends to leave early. After an hour, after they left, my father came home drunk as hell. He could barely stand. I avoided going in front of him, but he came to my room, banging on the door open, leaving me terrified. He then entered the room and then grabbed me by my hair and pulled me out of my bed and started dragging me downstairs towards the living room. I was hurt, I was crying, but he didn't listen to anything. He then threw me on the floor and picked up a rod and started beating me. He hit me everywhere, leaving my face alone, but the actual scars were not to be seen on the face. It was my soul that was hurt. He kept hitting me with the rod wherever he liked and abused me, telling me to stay away from people. I was terrified to my soul. I was crying in pain. I was horrified. I still am. He hit me so hard that it's difficult for me to write even. I wish I hadn't been born, then this day would have never come. I'm not going to make any friends if this is what I'll be rewarded with. I can't even express what I'm feeling now. I'll never celebrate my birthday again, nor will I tell anyone about it. I wish my mother was still alive today and miss her. I guess this was the worst day of my life.

1 NOVEMBER, 2005

Today was the most peaceful day of my life so far. My father had to go out of town for work, leaving Radhika and me alone at home. For the first time, it felt like we were free and we can live without any fear. We danced, laughed, talked until late at night, and ate whatever we wanted. We even went out to the garden, the same garden where my mother used to take us when we were kids. It's the only place that I remember being associated with my mother's memories.

22 MAY, 2006

It's been a while since I have written anything. I feel like I have become more silent with each passing day. I don't talk much, and I keep everything to myself, not even at school. I mainly concentrate on my studies. I have made a friend, though. Not a close one, but I talk to her sometimes in school. Her name is Kanika. Our conversations are mainly about school-related stuff. I don't want to share about my personal life with her, but she's still a good friend of mine.

Besides having a new friend, nothing has changed much at home. My father still doesn't talk to me, and I don't want to talk to him either. He continues to beat us for every small thing he sees as an opportunity. I guess I have gotten used to it because there is nothing I can do about it at this time. All I can do is wait for my studies to be over and start a new life away from this place, away from this monster. I want to study hard and achieve whatever I want to for my own benefit, for Radhika, and to make my mother proud. After all this time, I haven't lost any hope. I know one day I'll soon get out of this place and find a new home for me and my sister. After all, life is all about making it through the hard days without losing hope and wishing for a better future, and working hard in order to achieve that. One thing I can say for sure is that I'll never lose hope, as it's the only thing that keeps me going. I hope everything goes well

Aanchal...

15 MARCH, 2007

A very strange thing happened today. I was late for school and had to stand outside for punishment. One of my classmates was also late, and he came and stood behind me. Suddenly, he leaned in and whispered "HAPPY BIRTHDAY" in my ears. I was shocked because I haven't told anyone about my birthday, and no one has ever seemed to care much about me. But this guy, Aditya, how could he know that it was my birthday today? And why did he wish me a happy birthday? I've never really talked to him. He's a notorious kind of guy. I think I saw him once outside my house in the garden where Radhika and I go to play whenever my father is out of town. I saw him there playing, but I never really paid attention to him at that time. I was busy enjoying my own hours of freedom.

It feels good when someone wishes you a happy birthday, as if they care. These little things show how much one person cares about another. I remember my mom used to remember little things about me and Radhika, like what we always told her, anything meaningful or senseless. She remembered it all. After all, she was our mom. How could she forget what her children shared with her?

29 MAY, 2007

It's been a couple of weeks since my birthday incident. I think Aditya is trying to talk to me somehow. He deliberately asks for anything he can just to talk to me. I might be wrong, but I don't think I am. He even visits the garden every day. I can see him playing right now, too. He's down there pretending to play, but actually he's looking at my room's window.
I don't get what exactly he wants from me?

How did he find out it was my home after all?
Is he following me?
I hope not!
But if he's following me he's going to get me in great trouble if father finds out.
What does he exactly want from me?
I guess ignoring him is the best way to avoid any drama. I should concentrate on my own studies. But... should i ask him about his strange behaviour towards me lately? No i don't think so that's great idea. I guess i should just forget about this matter...

I really don't know what I'm feeling today. When I reached school, I saw Kanika calling me from a distance and running towards me as I entered the class. I was confused by her behaviour. She started blabbering, and I was getting confused. I asked her to calm down and tell me slowly everything. Then she told me that she had heard from some of our classmates that Aditya liked me a lot and was in love with me. I was shocked by her statement. I didn't know how to react. I was angry and hurt at the same time, as everyone now will think that I had done some sort of crime. Everyone would point at me and would making fun of me. Thinking this gave me panic attacks and all the anger and hurt emotions piled up at the same time, and I started crying. Kanika was trying to calm me down, but my tears were constantly rolling down, as I wasn't getting what was happening to me. Then I saw Aditya coming towards me. I think he was trying to tell me something, but I was so angry at him that I warned him to stay the hell away from me and told him to never bother me again, or I would complain about him. As I told him to do so, he stood there frozen, watching me cry, and then I left the class, ran outside to calm myself. For the whole day, I kept quiet and didn't talk to anyone.

I came home lost, constantly thinking about what Kanika had told me about Aditya's feelings for me. This is the first time in a while that someone has shown some affection towards me, and what did I do? I didn't really understand what to do about it. I mean, I never thought about such things. I was constantly busy working on my future goals and everything, and with the situations at home with my father, I never really thought that someone would like me. I don't know what to do at this time. I think telling him to stay away from me was probably the best thing I did for both of us.

9 AUGUST, 2007

Today I'm lost. Lost in thoughts that I don't understand. It's been a few months since I found out that Aditya loves me. And I haven't really understood what changed in me after that day. I have been thinking about him ever since, even though I try to force myself not to. He constantly tries to talk to me, but I still ignore him. He sometimes shows concern about things, but I even ignore that. I have no idea what to do in this kind of situation. I wish my mom were here so I could talk to her about it.

I see him everyday playing outside in the garden. But i think he's more interested in looking at me window than in playing. He seems concerned. What am i thinking? Aanchal! he's just another guy. You should not think about him at all.

But i think he's making every effort to talk to me, to get closer to me.

I never saw him studying. Never ever. But a couple of days ago, he started sitting in the front row and paid attention in every lecture. Even though he was paying attention to the teacher, he never stopped looking at me. Maybe it was just to impress me. But he actually paid attention to the lectures. I mean, the guy who always failed in every test scored good marks today. I was really shocked. But I behaved as if it didn't bother me at all. And I saw him cheer for me when I was declared first in the test. It actually felt good. Except, Radhika nobody has ever appreciated or cheered me on my success. Although it was just a test, it actually felt great.

If i'm not wrong, i think i have actually started to like this guy. But it's better for me to stay away from him because if father finds about him he's definitely gonna hurt me. So it's for my own good to stay away. I'll keep on ignoring him.

10 SEPTEMBER, 2007

The school fest is on its way. I'll participate again this year in the quiz in order to get a scholarship for my higher studies. I'm really excited as this is the thing that i love the most. Let's just hope i get a good team to pair up with in order to win the quiz.

12 September, 2007

When will Aditya stop following me around?

I really don't know how to deal with him? I found out today that he is going to participate in the quiz. and he's gonna be teamed up with me. I don't know what to do about it. I ignore him all the time but he keeps on finding ways to talk to me, to get closer. I don't know what to do with him but i'll not be participating in the quiz if he's going to do so. I mean one day i think i like this guy but then does something so stupid that make me think what kind of a jerk he is.

18 September, 2007

He hit me again today. And it was the worst of all times. I feel broken. I'm hurt. I don't know when will this stop.

Father somehow found about me not participating in the school quiz. He came home drunk and angry and started calling me down and as soon as i came down he slapped me hard. he kept on doing that for a few minutes, i cried a lot but it didn't affect him and he hit me and left the house.

I felt disheartened. I felt lonely. I was in pain so i went up to the attic to get some fresh air. But then i saw Aditya standing there in the garden, frozen as if he had seen some ghost. I think he saw father hitting me. And now i feel so ashamed. I feel so bad that somebody saw what i have been going through. I hope he doesn't tell about this to anyone at school because i won't be able to handle that look on everybody's face. But Aditya didn't leave the garden even after seeing that. He was constantly looking at my window. He looked concerned. He didn't saw me looking at him from the attic. But i could see him clearly.

Was he really concerned? He really cares that much about me. I don't know. I think i'm just going to take a couple of days off school in order to get over what happened today.

21 September, 2007

Today was the best day of my life. For the first

time, I realized that someone cares about me so much, that somebody loves me so much. I felt so great that I can't even find words to describe what I'm feeling right now.

When I reached school today, I sat at my seat and started doing my own work. After some time, I saw Aditya coming towards me. I ignored him and continued with my own work. He came up to me and asked me why I didn't come to school for a few days. As usual, I ignored him.

But then he handed me a medium-sized canvas sheet and told me to open it. As I opened it, I saw a painting. It was a very beautiful painting. It was of me. He had painted me. I could see the garden that I love and then there was me, running there in my red dress with a big smile. I saw a cheerful me, a different me. I don't know what I loved about that painting, but it made me feel complete. I felt so happy that I smiled looking at it and told him that he's crazy. To which, he replied that his parents call him Aditya. Such a stupid answer, but I was so lost in the painting that I just kept on smiling.

He gave me the painting to keep it with me. I can't stop looking at it. It's just so beautiful. Everything about it looks so pure and complete in itself. I think i fell in love with him the moment i saw his painting

Yes.

I love this guy.

I love him.

I love Aditya.

And the garden in which he painted me is my LOVE GARDEN. The garden where i found my love.

I'm in love and I'll love him forever.

1 November, 2007

Ever since I fell in love with Aditya, I haven't been able to stop thinking about him. We don't talk, but we at least share some smiles. I really want to talk to him and tell him how much I love him. I also want to ask him how he really feels about me and as I want to share my future with him. I want to be his everything and for him to be the same for me. I want to share a lifetime of happiness with him, and I can't keep these feelings to myself anymore. That's why I have decided to tell him everything about how I feel.

9 November, 2007

I'm dying inside. I don't know what really happened. Ever since i expressed my felling for Aditya through that letter he has been ignoring me. What does

he want now? Firstly, he showed his love through that painting of his's and now he's been behaving so strangely as if i never existed for him. What does this mean? I love him so much. I can't see the way he's behaving. Why is he doing this to me? i feel like crying. I feel like going up to him and asking him what is actually going on in his mind? Why is he playing such games with me? Why?
I love him so much.

14 November, 2007

He kissed me today and for the first time he said that he love me, and I slapped him. he forced me to do so. i don't understand him. he's been ignoring me ever since my letter and asking me today why am i playing games with him. i mean what did i do? Expressing my feelings were just a game for him. i can't understand what is going on. I really need to talk to him about it and tomorrow I will. Tomorrow either we are going to be together or this thing would end right here because i can't take it anymore. I love him and I'm going to tell him everything about it and ask him what he wants.

I LOVE YOU ADITYA and i want to be yours forever and ever. (Last entry)

And that was all. That was her last entry in her

journal. I don't know what to feel. Should I be happy that she loved me or sad because I lost her before anything could happen between us? I am dying inside. My heart is aching and I feel like it will burst anytime with the pain I am feeling right now. She was in so much pain with all the things going on in her life, yet she chose to love me. Her story made me sadder and I want to love her more, but I can't. She is gone, gone away forever. I couldn't even share her sorrows with her. All I ever wanted was to make her happy, but I didn't realize that my loving her would get her into so much trouble and she had to lose her life. I wish I had never seen her in that garden, the one she called her 'love garden.' I just wish I had never met her, never loved her so much, and never craved her attention. Now she is gone and I can't bear that. I don't know what to do with my life anymore. She was my inspiration and she was the one I wanted to do anything for. I feel devastated from the inside. I feel hollow.

15 MARCH, 2018

"It's been 10 years since I left this place. Coming back here reminds me of all the pain that I went through when Aanchal died. Though 10 years have passed, there hasn't been a single day when I don't think about her. It feels like it was yesterday when I saw her for the first time playing in her 'love garden.' She looked so pure and full of life. The memories of that day are still fresh in my mind, and as I think about that day, I can still feel the pain of losing her.

After she died, I was so depressed that I didn't even come out of my room. My parents were worried, so they sent me to Chicago to continue my studies there so that I stay away from her memories. And it kind of worked. I kept myself so busy there. I was just focused on my career, just like she wanted to do in her life. She showed me somehow what life actually means. Even after everything I had been through, I never lost hope. It took me a while to understand this, but soon I realized it what career I want to pursue in my life. And then I became what I wanted to be

AN ARTIST.

It was where my passion lied, and I found it just because of her. And whatever I am today is just for her. I wish she was here with me to share my success, but unfortunately, it's not so. I still love her a lot and I'll never forget her until my last breath.

HAPPY BIRTHDAY AANCHAL.

(somebody calls Aditya from behind)

AANCHAL is calling me now. I can sense Aanchal's excitement as we prepare to catch our flight, even though she has no idea where we're going. In the past, I always had an excuse for why I didn't want to visit my hometown – I didn't want to confront the painful memories that lingered there. It's been ten years since I last visited the place where I lost my love. I know it will be a hauntingly beautiful experience, one that I'm both excited and nervous to experience. But this time is different – this trip isn't for me, it's for Aanchal. As I gather my things and prepare to leave, I can't help but feel a sense of anticipation for the journey ahead.

I named my daughter Aanchal. She just turned five. It's a coincidence or I don't know what to call it as she was born on the same day as her. If it hasn't been so, I still would have named her Aanchal. She reminds me of her sometimes and now she is my life, my beautiful daughter Aanchal. I would do anything to keep her safe and happy and I can never think of hurting her in any way at all. I want to give all the happiness in her life that she deserves (the happiness that I couldn't give her).

I used to think that loving someone meant they had to be by my side. But I learned that this isn't always the case. Distance and even death cannot diminish the power of love. After Aanchal's passing, I believed that I would never love again. However, I was wrong. I discovered that love can come back in unexpected ways, and in my case, it returned in the form of my daughter.

INDIA

Upon arriving in India, the first thing I did was visit the garden. As I stand in front of the garden, memories flood back to me – memories of a time long gone. It's been ten years since I last saw this place, and yet it feels as though no time has passed at all. The vibrant colours of the flowers, the soothing sound of the water fountain, the gentle rustling of the leaves – it's all so familiar. I stand here, waiting and hoping, feeling my heart beat faster with each passing moment. This place is just as serene and peaceful as it was when I last visited. I can't help but feel a sense of nostalgia as I look around, remembering the time I spent here, and longing for a glimpse of the woman I loved. I think back to the first time I saw her in this very garden, wearing a red dress and looking so beautiful. It was the day I fell in love with her, and even though she's not here with me now, I still miss her and want her in my life. Tears well up in my eyes as I sit here, lost in memories of love and longing.

As I stood outside the house, lost in thought, Aanchal, approached me and asked if I wanted to play with her in the garden. I wiped away my tears and agreed, trying to push aside my thoughts of the past. We spent the next 30 minutes running around and having fun, enjoying each other's company. Eventually, I realized that we are running late for a function and decided to head back home.

I have been invited as chief guest by the mayor of my city as they want to felicitate me for my success and for my contribution in the field of arts. As, one of my paintings have fetched me 100,000$ and has become a symbol of love.

The event was scheduled to begin at 8:00pm and we arrived right on time. I took a seat at the front of the room with my daughter by my side. Before long, the mayor of the city stepped up to the podium to give a speech honoring me.

"We would like to call upon the stage Mr. Aditya Thakur. It is an honour to recognize the excellence of Mr. Aditya in the field of arts. He has consistently demonstrated exceptional talent and dedication to his craft, consistently producing high-quality work that has garnered widespread acclaim. His contributions to the arts community have been invaluable, and he serves as an inspiration to all those who aspire to greatness in this field. He is truly a shining example of what it means to be a dedicated and skilled artist, and it is a privilege to recognize his many accomplishments and contributions.

Without further delay, the mayor unveiled the masterpiece to the eager crowd. The masterpiece was called "LOVE GARDEN".

The unveiling was met with cheers and applause as people marvelled at the incredible work of art. I could sense Aanchal appreciating me with her loudest cheer in the hall.

The End

www.ingramcontent.com/pod-product-compliance
Lightning Source LLC
LaVergne TN
LVHW010703200726
843507LV00011B/1986